REACHING FOR THE STARS

BONNIE BLAIR
Five-time Gold Medal Winner

Bob Italia

Published by Abdo & Daughters, 4940 Viking Drive, Suite 622, Edina, Minnesota 55435.

Library bound edition distributed by Rockbottom Books, Pentagon Tower, P.O. Box 36036, Minneapolis, Minnesota 55435.

Copyright © 1994 by Abdo Consulting Group, Inc., Pentagon Tower, P.O. Box 36036, Minneapolis, Minnesota 55435 USA. International copyrights reserved in all countries. No part of this book may be reproduced in any form without written permission from the publisher.

Printed in the United States.

Cover Photo credit: Bettmann
Interior Photo credits: Bettmann

Edited by Rosemary Wallner

Library of Congress Cataloging-in-Publication Data

Italia, Bob, 1955-
    Bonnie Blair / Bob Italia.
        p.   cm. -- (Reaching For The Stars)
    ISBN 1-56239-341-3
    1. Blair, Bonnie, 1964-   --Juvenile literature. 2. Skaters--United States--Biography--Juvenile literature. 3. Speed skating--Juvenile literature. 4. Olympics--Juvenile literature. I. Title. II. Series.
    GV850.B63I83   1994
    796.91'4'092--dc20   94-23383
    [B]   CIP
                                                                                         AC

TABLE OF CONTENTS

BONNIE BLURR 4
A YOUNG SKATER 6
LEARNING TO SKATE 8
COMPETITIVE SKATING 9
OLYMPIC DREAMS 10
RAISING FUNDS 12
MAKING THE TEAM 13
BUTTE 14
REACHING THE TOP 16
WORLD RECORDS 17
OLYMPIC FAVORITE 18
TAKING A BREAK 21
RETURNING TO FORM 23
ALBERTVILLE 24
LILLEHAMMER 26
TAKING HER PLACE IN OLYMPIC HISTORY 29
NOW WHAT? 30

BONNIE BLURR

The best female speed skater ever produced by the United States is Bonnie Blair. She won one gold medal at the 1988 Winter Olympics in Calgary, Canada, two at the 1992 Winter Games in Albertville, France, and two at the Winter Games in Lillehammer.

Blair is the only woman from the United States ever to win gold medals in consecutive Winter Olympics and the only one to win three gold medals overall in the Winter Games. She is also just the second woman from the United States to win two gold medals in the same Olympics and the first female speed skater from any nation to win consecutive golds in the five-hundred-meter race.

At five feet, four inches tall and 130 pounds, Blair is small for a speed skater. But she makes up for her lack of size with superior skating technique and mental toughness.

Peter Mueller, the coach of the American speed skating team and himself a former gold medalist in the sport, said that

USA speed skater Bonnie Blair races to win the gold medal in the women's 1,000 Meters competition at the XVII Winter Olympic Games in Hamar, Norway.

Blair is "the best technician in the world over the sprint distance [five hundred and one thousand meters], man or woman. She's real dynamic; she gets everything out of her stroke. It's like she was born on the ice."

Growing up in a large, close-knit family helped Blair develop a positive mental attitude. This enabled her to endure years of rigorous training. "We were always a happy family, Blair said. "There were very few times that I was angry or mad, and it's this outlook that I brought with me to sports.... If I put in the physical work and my competitor does the same kind of training, but doesn't have the strong positive mental outlook that I do, then she's going to be beaten."

A YOUNG SKATER

Bonnie Kathleen Blair was born on March 18, 1964 in Cornwall, New York. She was the youngest of the six children of Charlie Blair, a civil engineer, and Eleanor Blair, a real-estate agent. Her parents had intended to have only five children, but seven years after the birth of her fifth child, Eleanor Blair discovered she was pregnant again.

"She was my do-it-yourself grandchild as far as some of my friends were concerned," said Eleanor Blair, who was forty-six when Bonnie was born.

On the afternoon Eleanor went into labor with Bonnie, Charlie was scheduled to work as a timer at a skating meet in which several of the Blair children were competing. Not wanting to miss the meet, he drove his wife to the hospital, dropped her off, and continued on to the rink. "He knew he was going to have to wait," Blair said. "He figured it might as well be at the rink." During the meet, the public address announcer issued the following statement: "Looks like the Blairs have another skater."

Despite the wide gap in age between Bonnie and her siblings (she is twenty-three years younger than Charlie Jr., the oldest Blair child), she "fit right in," Eleanor Blair said.

LEARNING TO SKATE

Charlie and Eleanor Blair had both enjoyed ice skating as youngsters. One Christmas before Blair was born they gave three of their children figure skates as gifts. All the Blair children soon became interested in skating. But each preferred skating fast to performing figure-skating maneuvers.

When Blair was two years old, her father took a job as a sales manager for a concrete company in Champaign, Illinois. The family relocated there. Shortly after the move, the older Blair children took Blair to an ice rink for the first time. Her feet were so small that her brothers and sisters had to leave her shoes on when they put on her skates. "I can't even remember learning how to skate," Blair said. "It comes almost as naturally to me as walking."

A speed skating hotbed, the university town of Champaign provided the Blair children with the facilities, coaching, and competition needed to excel at the sport. The Blairs entered competitive speed skating at the suggestion of a coach who saw several of them whizzing around the University of Illinois rink. Soon the entire clan was driving to regional speed skating meets on winter weekends.

COMPETITIVE SKATING

Four of Blair's five siblings went on to win national speed skating titles. Blair entered her first competition at the age of four, winning preliminary heats in her age division. By the time she was six, she was winning races against girls three and four years older. At seven, she competed in the Illinois state championships.

Blair's fledgling career received a big boost in 1979. That's when Cathy Priestner Faminow moved to Champaign to coach speed skating. Faminow, who had won a silver medal in speed skating for Canada at the 1976 Winter Olympics, worked with Blair on her technique and got permission for her to use the University of Illinois rink for early morning practice sessions.

"Cathy was around at exactly the right time in my life," Blair recalled. "She was a technical skater, like I am, and she had a big effect on me. She got me to work on my skating all year round instead of just during the winter months."

OLYMPIC DREAMS

Later in 1979 Blair competed in her first Olympic-style race, and her time was good enough to qualify her for the United States Olympic trials. Only fifteen years old, she narrowly missed making the 1980 United States Olympic speed skating team.

At the 1980 Olympic Games in Lake Placid, New York, American speed skater Eric Heiden became one of Blair's heroes after he won the gold medal in each of the five men's events. In 1980 and 1981, Blair trained while attending Champaign's Centennial High School. In addition to competing in speed skating events in Champaign, she took part in high school track and gymnastics.

The type of speed skating in which Blair then competed, pack skating, differs from Olympic-style skating. In pack skating, several skaters race each other on 110-meter ovals, in Olympic skating, skaters race against the clock on four-hundred-meter ovals, with just two skaters racing at a time.

In the early 1980s, the United States had only two refrigerated 400 meter speed skating tracks—one at Lake Placid and the other at West Allis, Wisconsin, which was open only a few months a year.

In 1982 Cathy Faminow advised Bonnie Blair to train in Europe, where there are many more Olympic-sized rinks, and to compete on the European winter speed skating circuit to improve her chances in the 1984 Olympics. Blair was eager to go to Europe, but she lacked the money to finance the trip.

The United States Speed Skating Federation informed Blair that it did not have the revenue to sponsor American athletes competing abroad. Her parents were also unable to provide her with any financial assistance, since her father had recently retired.

RAISING FUNDS

Forced to raise her own funds, Blair sought help from several Champaign businessmen, each of whom merely wished her good luck. With time running out, she turned to Gerry Schweighart, a Champaign police officer and the father of one of her high school friends.

Schweighart, a veteran fund-raiser, had told Blair to come to him if she ever needed financial help. After Blair informed him that she had about a month to raise the $7,000 she needed to compete in the 1982-83 World Cup speed skating events, the Champaign police department held a series of raffles and bake sales in her behalf. Thanks to the police department's efforts and a $1,500 donation by the professional basketball player Jack Sikma, a former fraternity brother of Blair's brother Rob, Blair was able to raise the necessary funds. While competing in Europe, Blair earned her high school degree by correspondence course.

MAKING THE TEAM

Blair made the 1984 United States Olympic team and competed in the five hundred meters at that year's Winter Games in Sarajevo, Yugoslavia. She finished eighth in a competition dominated by speed skaters from what was then East Germany.

USA speed skater Bonnie Blair on her way to winning the gold at Albertville, France 1992.

"I was in total awe the whole time," Blair said. "It was an eye-opening experience. Just my two sisters and my mother went with me, not the Blair Bunch you saw here (maybe 60 relatives and friends decked out in Bonnie sweatshirts and golden ball caps). I got all choked up. I was in awe the whole time. I mean, I'd sit in the duling hall with Scott Hamilton and the Mahre brothers, Steve and Phil. My mouth would be on the ground. I'd sit five hours in the cafeteria, saying, 'Hey, I'm here with them. This is just amazing.' "

Blair received a financial boost when $1.3 million in surplus funds from the 1984 Summer Olympics, in Los Angeles, was distributed to the United States Speed Skating Federation. The Champaign police department continued to raise funds for Blair. They sold bumper stickers and T-shirts that read: "Champaign Policemen's Favorite Speeder: Olympian Bonnie Blair."

BUTTE

Bonnie Blair began to improve her skating times greatly under the tutelage of Mike Crowe, then the coach of the United States national speed skating team. She has credited

Crowe, who oversaw a training facility in Butte, Montana, with playing a major role in helping her refine her technique.

During the middle and late 1980s, Butte became a second home for Blair. She lived with the family of her boyfriend, David Silk, also an Olympic speed skater. He convinced her that the way to greatness was through hard work and improved training habits.

In 1987, Blair admitted that until 1985 she had been "lazy about training. If I had something else I wanted to do, I did it.... But the last two years, if I missed a workout, I felt guilty about it and made it up." Blair's training regimen included long skating sessions in the morning, weight training, running, biking, and roller skating.

Blair's career in pack skating peaked in 1986, when she won the world championship in short-track skating, a type of pack skating that features a 111-meter track and the use of specially constructed skates. From then on, she directed almost all of her energy toward Olympic-style skating.

Her long involvement in pack skating was not without

benefits, however, since it taught her how to get off to fast starts and thus avoid collisions. "You don't collide with people if you're in front of them," she said.

REACHING THE TOP

Blair's breakthrough to the upper bracket of international speed skating came at the 1986 World Sprint Championships. There, in the five-hundred-meter competition, she tied for second place with Christa Rothenburger of East Germany, the 1984 Olympic gold medalist in that event.

Encouraged by her success, Blair redoubled her training efforts. During a one hundred-day period in the 1986-87 season, a whirlwind travel schedule took her from the Netherlands to Wisconsin to Switzerland to New York to Canada to Finland to Norway to what was then West Germany to the Netherlands again and, finally, to the former Soviet Union.

WORLD RECORDS

On her second trip to the Netherlands, Blair skated the five hundred meters in 39.43 seconds, breaking the world record, which was then held by Karen Kania of East Germany. A week later, at a 500 meter race in the former Soviet Union, Blair turned in an unofficial time of 39.28. She lost only one five hundred-meter race during the 1986-87 season. But that one defeat cost her the World Sprint championship, in which she placed second to Kania. She did win the World Cup championship, however.

In December 1987, at a World Cup event in Calgary, Canada, the site of the 1988 Winter Olympics, Rothenburger defeated Blair in the 500 meters, setting a new world record with a time of 39.39 seconds. But Blair refused to allow the defeat to dent her confidence. "No matter what happened that day, she won't beat me again at Calgary," Blair said. "I still will win the gold medal."

OLYMPIC FAVORITE

Blair was ranked as the favorite to win the five hundred-meter event at the Calgary Games. She was also considered a contender for a medal in the 1,000 meter and 1,500-meter races.

Helping Blair to combat the pressure in Calgary was a support group of about twenty family members and friends. On the morning of the 500 meter event, Blair, fearing her nervousness would cause an upset stomach, ate a peanut butter-and-jelly sandwich. Rothenburger, skating two pairs before Blair, turned up the pressure by finishing with a time of 39.12 seconds to break her own world record.

Bolstered by the memory of a faster practice lap earlier in the week, Blair knew she had what it took to beat Rothenburger. When the gun sounded, she burst away from the starting line in what she later called her best start ever, covering the initial one hundred meters in 10.55 seconds. "My first turn wasn't as good as I would have liked, but the rest of the race was perfect," she said.

Bonnie Blair raises her arms and shouts with joy after setting a new world record and winning a gold medal at the Olympic Games in Calgary, Canada, 1988.

Blair zipped through the course in 39.10 seconds, thus beating Rothenburger by two-hundredths of a second and setting a new world record. If Blair and Rothenburger had been racing head-to-head, Blair's margin of victory would have been less than one foot.

Blair's time in the five hundred held up for the gold medal, and she was moved to tears while listening to the national anthem on the victory stand. She also captured a bronze medal in the one thousand meters, becoming the only athlete from the United States to win more than one medal at the Calgary games.

Bonnie Blair accepting the gold medal at Calgary, 1988.

Blair's teammates honored her achievement by nominating her to carry the American flag at the closing ceremonies. After she returned to the United States she received a host of endorsement offers. To field them she hired Players Professional Management of Champaign. On April 27, 1988, Blair attended a state dinner at the White House for Canadian prime minister Brian Mulroney.

TAKING A BREAK

In August 1988 Bonnie Blair left Champaign and moved back to Butte, where she enrolled at Montana College of Mineral Science and Technology. Cutting back on her training, she did not return to the ice until November and skipped the season's first two World Cup events. She did win the overall title at the World Sprint Championships for the first time, however, in 1989.

That same year, trying to duplicate the crossover success of other speed skaters, including Christa Rothenburger, Blair took up competitive bicycle racing. She made the United States women's cycling team but soon gave up the sport.

Despite a scaled-down training program in skating, Blair finished second at the 1990 World Sprint Championships. Largely because of a bout with bronchitis and the outbreak of the Persian Gulf war, which forced her to leave Europe prematurely, Blair finished third in the 1991 World Sprints. She was also bothered by the frequent unavailability of her coach, Mike Crowe, who had taken a second job as head of junior development for the United States Speed Skating Federation.

Partly at Blair's insistence, Crowe was replaced as coach of the United States Olympic speed skating team by Peter Mueller, the 1976 Olympic gold medalist in the one thousand meters. "Mike [Crowe] was very good at helping me find my rhythm, but I'd find it and he would have to leave again," Blair said. "The change in coaches definitely helps. Change is always good at keeping you fresh."

RETURNING TO FORM

Bonnie Blair returned to full-time speed skating training in the summer of 1991. Because she had contracts with several United States Olympic Committee sponsors and two other companies, she was no longer dependent on the financial support of the Champaign police department. She also hired a new agency, Advantage International, to represent her.

"Doing other things in the years in between the Olympics was good both as a break and because it helped me realize I didn't want to look back and go, 'What if?' About 1992," Blair said.

In the first two World Cup events of the 1991-92 season, Blair won two five-hundred-meter races and two one-thousand-meter races. She entered the 1992 Winter Olympics in Albertville, France, as the favorite in the former event and a leading contender in the latter. Although Karen Kania had retired, Christa Luding (the former Christa Rothenburger) and Ye Qiaobo of China loomed as tough competitors.

ALBERTVILLE

Unfavorable weather conditions made for a slow track at the Albertville rink. As she had been in 1988, Blair was cheered on by a large contingent of family and friends. She again calmed her pre-race jitters by consuming her old standby—a peanut butter-and-jelly sandwich.

On February 10 she easily won the five hundred meters with a time of 40.33 seconds (she dedicated the medal to her father, who had died in 1989). Four days later, with a time of one minute and 21.9 seconds, she took the one thousand meters by a narrow margin.

Following her triumph at Albertville, Blair appeared in a series of television commercials for McDonald's restaurants. Her picture was featured on boxes of Kellogg's Corn Flakes. She was also featured on a postage stamp in the small Caribbean nation of Saint Vincent and the Grenadines. Though some people thought she would retire, Blair stated her intention to compete in the 1994 Winter Olympics in Lillehammer, Norway.

USA speed skater Bonnie Blair shows her Olympic women's 1000 meters speed skating gold medal that she won at the 1992 Albertville, France, Winter Olympics.

LILLEHAMMER

After a decade on the ice, Blair had earned three Olympic gold medals. But Blair was a reluctant legend, hesitant to acknowledge her own place in the record books.

It was left to others to measure Bonnie Blair. No one at the Lillehammer Games did it better than the Chinese speed skater Yi Qiabo, who finished third in Blair's last Olympic race ever, the 1,000 meters. Yi said, "It is not easy to get medal, even the third-place one." She knew who she was up against.

Still, some people had their doubts. "People were telling me I was too old already," Blair said.

When they lit the torch for the Olympics, Blair felt the heat. "The Olympics are very special," she said. "I might not always be at the top, but during the Olympic years I have been skating very well. I don't know if there is something about the Olympics that gets me going a little bit more.... I do know you can't count on anything when it's an Olympics because the Olympics is that much different."

Bonnie Blair wins her second gold medal at the 1994 Olympic Games in Norway. Her determination is shown on her face.

At the advanced speed skating age of 29, Blair somehow had rediscovered the speed of her youth. Her 1,000-meter time of 1 minute, 18.74 seconds was her fastest since the 1988 Games at Calgary. She gave credit to Jansen, who won the men's 1,000 in world-record time.

"What Dan did in his race, get to 600 meters extremely fast, definitely won the race for him," she said. "And I wanted to do the same thing."

After doing 600 meters in a quick 46.9 seconds, Blair had only one thought: "Hold on for dear life that last lap." At the finish she told her coach, Nick Thometz, "I don't know if that's good enough, but that's all I had."

More than good enough, Blair finished 1.38 seconds ahead of the second-place skater, Anke Beier of Germany. "That shocked me," Blair said.

It was the greatest woman's victory margin in an Olympics 1,000. The gap between Blair and second place was greater than that between the second-place finisher and the 16th.

"Being able to come away from the Olympics winning five golds and one bronze is something I definitely would have never dreamed of," Blair said. That's one more gold than any American woman had won in the Olympics, summer or winter.

TAKING HER PLACE IN OLYMPIC HISTORY

With one gold medal at Calgary in 1988, two at Albertville in 1992 and two at Lillehammer, Blair passed diver Pat McCormack, swimmer Janet Evans and sprinter Evelyn Ashford. Only the speedskater Heiden, the hero of Lake Placid's 1980 Games, had won as many winter golds for America.

"But it only took him one week," said Blair of Heiden. "It took me six years."

As Blair's teammate Chantal Bailey said, "She's like [U.S. track star] Carl Lewis. She keeps going out and winning golds. You know, it took Dan Jansen 10 years to win one gold medal. She's won five. That tells you how great an athlete she is."

Despite all her accomplishments, Blair's most vivid memory was of Jansen's victory. "To see him with a world record with the whole world knowing that was a medal well-deserved, totally awesome . . . That memory will stay with me," she said.

NOW WHAT?

For Blair, who would retire after the 1995 World Championships in Milwaukee, these Olympics were her last. It was time to get on with the rest of her life.

Blair said that after her last victory at Calgary, it "was almost sad" because halfway through the national anthem she realized what the moment meant. She thought, "This is never going to happen to me again."

Then she took a victory lap in the darkened Viking Ship hall. She wore the gold medal and someone from the Blair Bunch passed her a golden ball cap. Laughing, she put it on.

Blair will finish college. She will think of marriage and children. But she was intent on finding a way to keep a hand in speed skating. "It is a sport I thoroughly love," she said. "It has brought me a lot of happiness, and I want to return that."

Bonnie wears the golden ball cap that was passed to her from her fans at the Winter Olympics in Lillehammer, Norway, 1994.

United States Olympic speed skating legend, Bonnie Blair.